One fish
two fish
red fish
blue fish

By Dr. Seuss

HarperCollins *Children's Books*

ISBN: 978-0-00-790828-8

© 1960, 1988 by Dr. Seuss Enterprises, L.P.
All Rights Reserved
A Beginner Book published by arrangement with
Random House Inc., New York, USA
First published in the UK 1960
This edition published in the UK 2003 by
HarperCollins*Children's Books,*
a division of HarperCollins*Publishers* Ltd
77-85 Fulham Palace Road
London W6 8JB

Visit our website at:
www.harpercollins.co.uk

Printed and bound in Hong Kong

From there to here,
from here to there,
funny things
are everywhere.

One fish

two fish

red fish

blue fish.

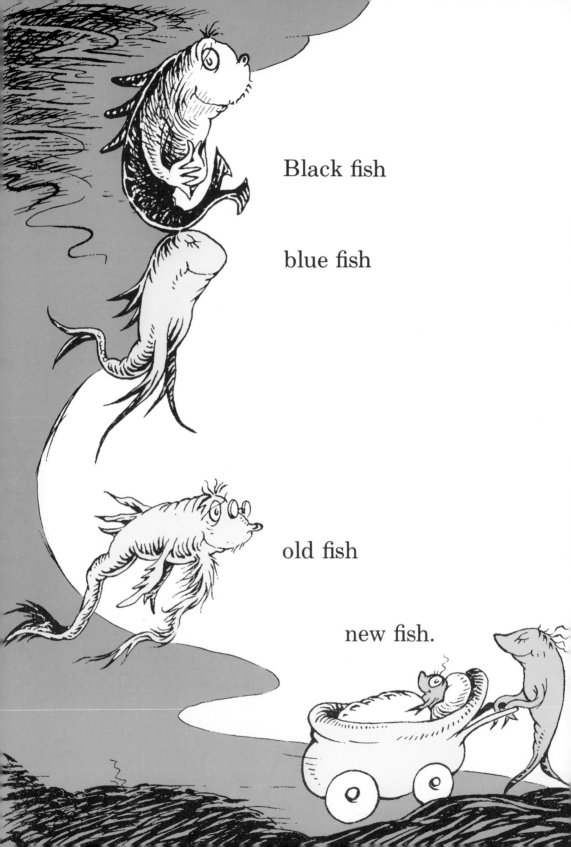

Black fish

blue fish

old fish

new fish.

This one has
a little star.

This one has a little car.
Say! what a lot
of fish there are.

Yes. Some are red. And some are blue.
Some are old. And some are new.

Some are sad.

And some are glad.

And some are very, very bad.

Why are they
sad and glad and bad?
I do not know.
Go ask your dad.

Some are thin.

And some are fat.
The fat one has
a yellow hat.

8

From there to here,
from here to there,
funny things
are everywhere.

9

Here are some
who like to run.
They run for fun
in the hot, hot sun.

Oh me! Oh my!

Oh me! Oh my!

What a lot

of funny things go by.

Some have two feet
and some have four.
Some have six feet
and some have more.

Where do they come from? I can't say.

But I bet they have come

a long, long way.

We see them come.

We see them go.

Some are fast.

And some are slow.

Some are high.

And some are low.

Not one of them
is like another.
Don't ask us why.
Go ask your mother.

Say!

Look at his fingers!

One, two, three . . .

How many fingers

do I see?

One, two, three, four,

five, six, seven,

eight, nine, ten.

He has eleven!

Eleven!

This is something new.

I wish I had

eleven, too!

Bump!

Bump!

Bump!

Did you ever ride a Wump?

We have a Wump

with just one hump.

But

we know a man

called Mr. Gump.

Mr. Gump has a seven hump Wump.

So . . .

if you like to go Bump! Bump!

just jump on the hump of the Wump of Gump.

Who am I?

My name is Ned.

I do not like

my little bed.

This is no good.

This is not right.

My feet stick out

of bed all night.

And when I pull them in,
Oh, dear!
My head sticks out of bed
up here!

We like our bike.
It is made for three.
Our Mike
sits up in back,
you see.

We like our Mike
and this is why:
Mike does all the work
when the hills get high.

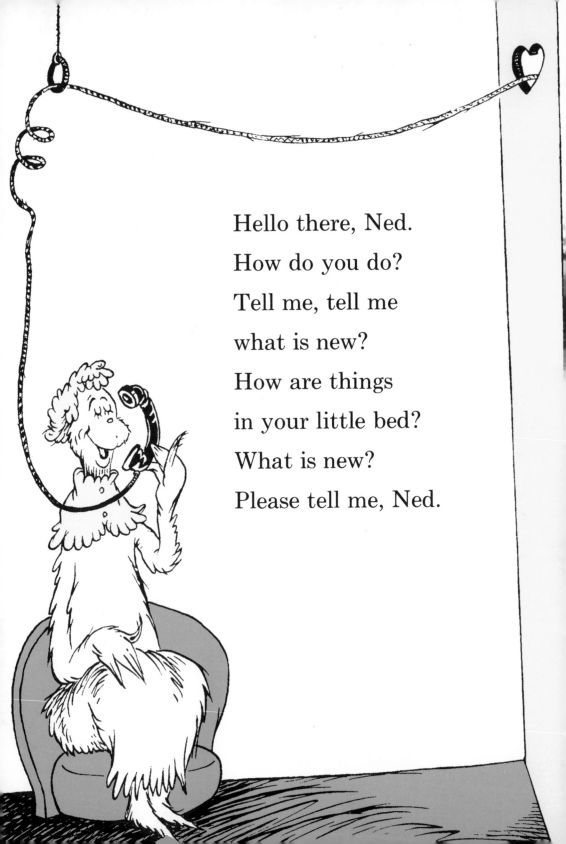

Hello there, Ned.
How do you do?
Tell me, tell me
what is new?
How are things
in your little bed?
What is new?
Please tell me, Ned.

I do not like

this bed at all.

A lot of things

have come to call.

A cow, a dog, a cat, a mouse.

Oh! what a bed! Oh! what a house!

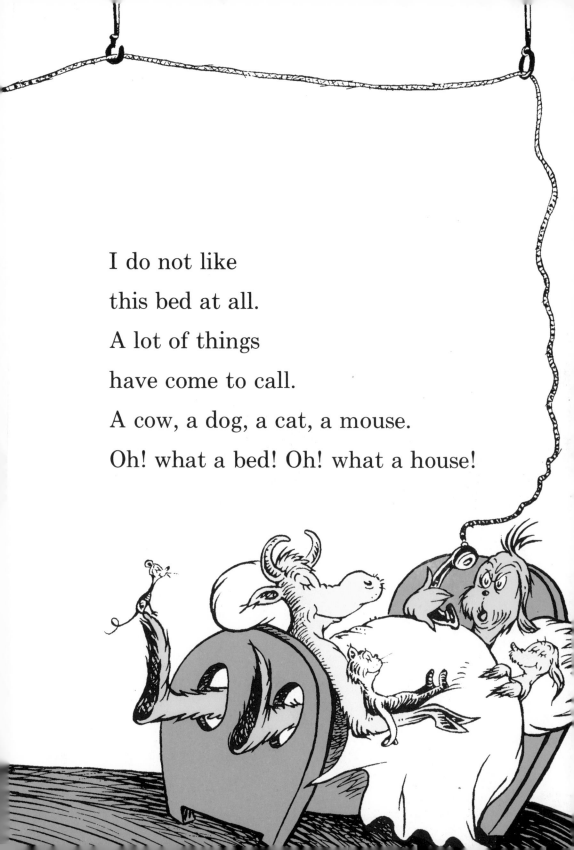

Oh, dear! Oh, dear!

I can not hear.

Will you please

come over near?

Will you please look in my ear?

There must be something there, I fear.

Say, look!

A bird was in your ear.

But he is out. So have no fear.

Again your ear can hear, my dear.

My hat is old.
My teeth are gold.

I have a bird
I like to hold.

My shoe is off.
My foot is cold.

My shoe is off.
My foot is cold.

I have a bird
I like to hold.

My hat is old.
My teeth are gold.

And now
my story
is all told.

We took a look.
We saw a Nook.
On his head
he had a hook.
On his hook
he had a book.
On his book
was "How to Cook."

We saw him sit
and try to cook.
He took a look
at the book on the hook.

But a Nook can't read,
so a Nook can't cook.
SO . . .
what good to a Nook
is a hook cook book?

The moon was out
and we saw some sheep.
We saw some sheep
take a walk in their sleep.

By the light of the moon,

by the light of a star,

they walked all night

from near to far.

I would never walk.

I would take a car.

I do not like
this one so well.
All he does
is yell, yell, yell.
I will not have this one about.
When he comes in
I put him out.

This one is
quiet as a mouse.
I like to have him
in the house.

At our house

we open cans.

We have to open

many cans.

And that is why

we have a Zans.

A Zans for cans

is very good.

Have you a Zans for cans?

You should.

I like to box.

How I like to box!

So, every day,

I box a Gox.

In yellow socks

I box my Gox.

I box in yellow

Gox box socks.

It is fun to sing
if you sing with a Ying.
My Ying can sing
like anything.

I sing high
and my Ying sings low,
and we are not too bad,
you know.

This one,
I think,
is called
a Yink.

He likes to wink,

he likes to drink.

He likes to drink, and drink, and drink.
The thing he likes to drink
is ink.
The ink he likes to drink is pink.
He likes to wink and drink pink ink.

SO . . .

if you have a lot of ink,
then you should get
a Yink, I think.

Hop! Hop! Hop!
I am a Yop.
All I like to do is hop
from finger top
to finger top.

I hop from left to right
and then . . .
Hop! Hop!
I hop right back again.

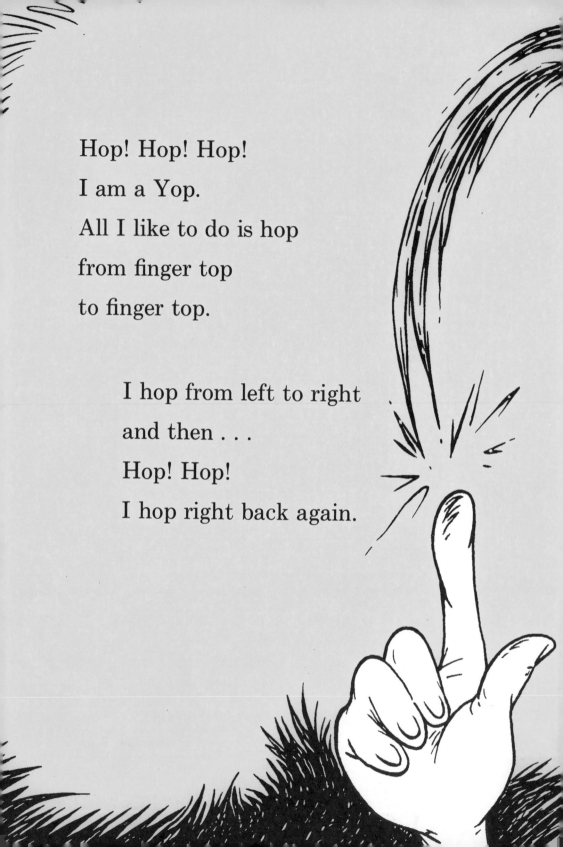